# Sylvia Of The Letters

By

Jerome K Jerome

British Library Cataloguing-in-Publication Data
A catalogue record for this book is available from the
British Library

# Jerome K. Jerome

Jerome Klapka Jerome was born in Walsall, England in 1859. Both his parents died while he was in his early teens, and he was forced to quit school to support himself. Jerome worked for a number of years collecting coal along railway tracks, before trying his hand at acting, journalism, teaching and soliciting. At long last, in 1885, he had some success with *On the Stage – and Off,* a comic memoir of his experiences with an acting troupe. Jerome produced a number of essays over the following years, and married in 1888, spending the honeymoon in "a little boat" on the Thames.

In 1889, Jerome published his most successful and best-remembered work, *Three Men in a Boat.* Featuring himself and two of his friends encountering humorous situations while floating down the Thames in a small boat, the book was an instant success, and has never been out of print. In fact, its popularity was such that the number of registered Thames boats went up fifty percent in the year following its publication. With the financial security provided by *Three Men in a Boat,* Jerome was able to dedicate himself fully to writing, producing eleven more novels and a number of anthologies of short fiction.

In 1926, Jerome published his autobiography, *My Life and Times.* He died a year later, aged 68.

Old Ab Herrick, so most people called him. Not that he was actually old; the term was an expression of liking rather than any reflection on his years. He lived in an old-fashioned house--old-fashioned, that is, for New York--on the south side of West Twentieth Street: once upon a time, but that was long ago, quite a fashionable quarter. The house, together with Mrs. Travers, had been left him by a maiden aunt. An "apartment" would, of course, have been more suitable to a bachelor of simple habits, but the situation was convenient from a journalistic point of view, and for fifteen years Abner Herrick had lived and worked there.

Then one evening, after a three days' absence, Abner Herrick returned to West Twentieth Street, bringing with him a little girl wrapped up in a shawl, and a wooden box tied with a piece of cord. He put the box on the table; and the young lady, loosening her shawl, walked to the window and sat down facing the room.

Mrs. Travers took the box off the table and put it on the floor--it was quite a little box--and waited.

"This young lady," explained Abner Herrick, "is Miss Ann Kavanagh, daughter of--of an old friend of mine."

"Oh!" said Mrs. Travers, and remained still expectant.

"Miss Kavanagh," continued Abner Herrick, "will be staying with us for--" He appeared to be uncertain of the length of Miss Kavanagh's visit. He left the sentence unfinished and took refuge in more pressing questions.

"What about the bedroom on the second floor? Is it ready? Sheets aired--all that sort of thing?"

"It can be," replied Mrs. Travers. The tone was suggestive of judgment reserved.

"I think, if you don't mind, Mrs. Travers, that we'd like to go to bed as soon as possible." From force of habit Abner S. Herrick in speaking employed as a rule the editorial "we." "We have been travelling all day and we are very tired. To-morrow morning--"

"I'd like some supper," said Miss Kavanagh from her seat in the window, without moving.

"Of course," agreed Miss Kavanagh's host, with a feeble pretence that the subject had been on the tip of his tongue. As a matter of fact, he really had forgotten all about it. "We might have it up here while the room is being got ready. Perhaps a little--"

"A soft boiled egg and a glass of milk, if you please, Mrs. Travers," interrupted Miss Kavanagh, still from her seat at the window.

"I'll see about it," said Mrs. Travers, and went out, taking the quite small box with her.

Such was the coming into this story of Ann Kavanagh at the age of eight years; or, as Miss Kavanagh herself would have explained, had the question been put to her, eight years and seven months, for Ann Kavanagh was a precise young lady. She was not beautiful--not then. She was much too sharp featured; the little pointed chin protruding into space to quite a dangerous extent. Her large dark eyes were her one redeeming feature. But the level brows above them were much too ready with their frown. A sallow complexion and nondescript hair deprived her of that charm of colouring on which youth can generally depend for attraction, whatever its faults of form. Nor could it truthfully be said that sweetness of disposition afforded compensation.

"A self-willed, cantankerous little imp I call her," was Mrs. Travers's comment, expressed after one of the many trials of strength between them, from which Miss Kavanagh had as usual emerged triumphant.

"It's her father," explained Abner Herrick, feeling himself unable to contradict.

"It's unfortunate," answered Mrs. Travers, "whatever it is."

To Uncle Ab himself, as she had come to call him, she could on occasion be yielding and affectionate; but that, as Mrs. Travers took care to point out to her, was a small thing to her credit.

"If you had the instincts of an ordinary Christian child," explained Mrs. Travers to her, "you'd be thinking twenty-four hours a day of what you could do to repay him for all his loving kindness to you; instead of causing him, as you know you do, a dozen heartaches in a week. You're an ungrateful little monkey, and when he's gone you'll--"

Upon which Miss Kavanagh, not waiting to hear more, flew upstairs and, locking herself in her own room, gave herself up to howling and remorse; but was careful not to emerge until she felt bad tempered again; and able, should opportunity present itself, to renew the contest with Mrs. Travers unhampered by sentiment.

But Mrs. Travers's words had sunk in deeper than that good lady herself had hoped for; and one evening, when Abner Herrick was seated at his desk penning a scathing indictment of the President for lack of firmness and decision on the tariff question, Ann, putting her thin arms round his neck and rubbing her little sallow face against his right-hand whisker, took him to task on the subject.

"You're not bringing me up properly--not as you ought to," explained Ann. "You give way to me too much, and you never scold me."

"Not scold you!" exclaimed Abner with a certain warmth of indignation. "Why, I'm doing it all--"

"Not what _I_ call scolding," continued Ann. "It's very wrong of you. I shall grow up horrid if you don't help me."

As Ann with great clearness pointed out to him, there was no one else to undertake the job with any chance of success. If Abner failed her, then she supposed there was no hope for her: she would end by becoming a wicked woman, and everybody, including herself, would hate her. It was a sad prospect. The contemplation of it brought tears to Ann's eyes.

He saw the justice of her complaint and promised to turn over a new leaf. He honestly meant to do so; but, like many another repentant sinner, found himself feeble before the difficulties of performance. He might have succeeded better had it not been for her soft deep eyes beneath her level brows.

"You're not much like your mother," so he explained to her one day, "except about the eyes. Looking into your eyes I can almost see your mother."

He was smoking a pipe beside the fire, and Ann, who ought to have been in bed, had perched herself upon one of the arms of his chair and was kicking a hole in the worn leather with her little heels.

"She was very beautiful, my mother, wasn't she?" suggested Ann.

Abner Herrick blew a cloud from his pipe and watched carefully the curling smoke.

"In a way, yes," he answered. "Quite beautiful."

"What do you mean, 'In a way'?" demanded Ann with some asperity.

"It was a spiritual beauty, your mother's," Abner explained. "The soul looking out of her eyes. I don't think it possible to imagine a more beautiful disposition than your mother's. Whenever I think of your mother," continued Abner after a pause, "Wordsworth's lines always come into my mind."

He murmured the quotation to himself, but loud enough to be heard by sharp ears. Miss Kavanagh was mollified.

"You were in love with my mother, weren't you?" she questioned him kindly.

"Yes, I suppose I was," mused Abner, still with his gaze upon the curling smoke.

"What do you mean by 'you suppose you were'?" snapped Ann. "Didn't you know?"

The tone recalled him from his dreams.

"I was in love with your mother very much," he corrected himself, turning to her with a smile.

"Then why didn't you marry her?" asked Ann. "Wouldn't she have you?"

"I never asked her," explained Abner.

"Why not?" persisted Ann, returning to asperity.

He thought a moment.

"You wouldn't understand," he told her.

"Yes, I would," retorted Ann.

"No, you wouldn't," he contradicted her quite shortly. They were both beginning to lose patience with one another. "No woman ever could."

"I'm not a woman," explained Ann, "and I'm very smart. You've said so yourself."

"Not so smart as all that," growled Abner. "Added to which, it's time for you to go to bed."

Her anger with him was such that it rendered her absolutely polite. It had that occasional effect upon her. She slid from the arm of his chair and stood beside him, a rigid figure of frozen femininity.

"I think you are quite right, Uncle Herrick. Good night!" But at the door she could not resist a parting shot:

"You might have been my father, and then perhaps she wouldn't have died. I think it was very wicked of you."

After she was gone Abner sat gazing into the fire, and his pipe went out. Eventually the beginnings of a smile stole to the corners of his mouth, but before it could spread any farther he dismissed it with a sigh.

Abner, for the next day or two, feared a renewal of the conversation, but Ann appeared to have forgotten it; and as time went by it faded from Abner's own memory. Until one evening quite a while later.

The morning had brought him his English mail. It had been arriving with some regularity, and Ann had noticed that Abner always opened it before his other correspondence. One letter he read through twice, and Ann, who was pretending to be reading the newspaper, felt that he was looking at her.

"I have been thinking, my dear," said Abner, "that it must be rather lonely for you here, all by yourself."

"It would be," answered Ann, "if I were here all by myself."

"I mean," said Abner, "without any other young person to talk to and--and to play with."

"You forget," said Ann, "that I'm nearly thirteen."

"God bless my soul," said Abner. "How time does fly!"

"Who is she?" asked Ann.

"It isn't a 'she,'" explained Abner. "It's a 'he.' Poor little chap lost his mother two years ago, and now his father's dead. I thought--it occurred to me we might put him up for a time. Look after him a bit. What do you think? It would make the house more lively, wouldn't it?"

"It might," said Ann.

She sat very silent, and Abner, whose conscience was troubling him, watched her a little anxiously. After a time she looked up.

"What's he like?" she asked.

"Precisely what I am wondering myself," confessed Abner. "We shall have to wait and see. But his mother--his mother," repeated Abner, "was the most beautiful woman I have ever known. If he is anything like she was as a girl--" He left the sentence unfinished.

"You have not seen her since--since she was young?" questioned Ann.

Abner shook his head. "She married an Englishman. He took her back with him to London."

"I don't like Englishmen," said Ann.

"They have their points," suggested Abner. "Besides, boys take after their mothers, they say." And Abner rose and gathered his letters together.

Ann remained very thoughtful all that day. In the evening, when Abner for a moment laid down his pen for the purpose of relighting his pipe, Ann came to him, seating herself on the corner of the desk.

"I suppose," she said, "that's why you never married mother?"

Abner's mind at the moment was much occupied with the Panama Canal.

"What mother?" he asked. "Whose mother?"

"My mother," answered Ann. "I suppose men are like that."

"What are you talking about?" said Abner, dismissing altogether the Panama Canal.

"You loved my mother very much," explained Ann with cold deliberation. "She always made you think of Wordsworth's perfect woman."

"Who told you all that?" demanded Abner.

"You did."

"I did?"

"It was the day you took me away from Miss Carew's because she said she couldn't manage me," Ann informed him.

"Good Lord! Why, that must be two years ago," mused Abner.

"Three," Ann corrected him. "All but a few days."

"I wish you'd use your memory for things you're wanted to remember," growled Abner.

"You said you had never asked her to marry you," pursued Ann relentlessly; "you wouldn't tell me why. You said I shouldn't understand."

"My fault," muttered Abner. "I forget you're a child. You ask all sorts of questions that never ought to enter your head, and I'm fool enough to answer you."

One small tear that had made its escape unnoticed by her was stealing down her cheek. He wiped it away and took one of her small paws in both his hands.

"I loved your mother very dearly," he said gravely. "I had loved her from a child. But no woman will ever understand the power that beauty has upon a man. You see we're built that way. It's Nature's lure. Later on, of course, I might have forgotten; but then it was too late. Can you forgive me?"

"But you still love her," reasoned Ann through her tears, "or you wouldn't want him to come here."

"She had such a hard time of it," pleaded Abner. "It made things easier to her, my giving her my word that I would always look after the boy. You'll help me?"

"I'll try," said Ann. But there was not much promise in the tone.

Nor did Matthew Pole himself, when he arrived, do much to help matters. He was so hopelessly English. At least, that was the way Ann put it. He was shy and sensitive. It is a trying combination. It made him appear stupid and conceited. A lonely childhood had rendered him unsociable, unadaptable. A dreamy, imaginative temperament imposed upon him long moods of silence: a liking for long solitary walks. For the first time Ann and Mrs. Travers were in agreement.

"A sulky young dog," commented Mrs. Travers. "If I were your uncle I'd look out for a job for him in San Francisco."

"You see," said Ann in excuse for him, "it's such a foggy country, England. It makes them like that."

"It's a pity they can't get out of it," said Mrs. Travers.

Also, sixteen is an awkward age for a boy. Virtues, still in the chrysalis state, are struggling to escape from their parent vices. Pride, an excellent quality making for courage and patience, still appears in the swathings of arrogance. Sincerity still expresses itself in the language of rudeness. Kindness itself is apt to be mistaken for amazing impertinence and love of interference.

It was kindness--a genuine desire to be useful, that prompted him to point out to Ann her undoubted faults and failings, nerved him to the task of bringing her up in the way she should go. Mrs. Travers had long since washed her hands of the entire business. Uncle Ab, as Matthew also called him, had proved himself a weakling. Providence, so it seemed to Matthew, must have been waiting impatiently for his advent. Ann at first thought it was some new school of humour. When she found he was serious she set herself to cure him. But she never did. He was too conscientious for that. The instincts of the guide, philosopher, and friend to humanity in general were already too strong in him. There were times when

Abner almost wished that Matthew Pole senior had lived a little longer.

But he did not lose hope. At the back of his mind was the fancy that these two children of his loves would come together. Nothing is quite so sentimental as a healthy old bachelor. He pictured them making unity from his confusions; in imagination heard the patter on the stairs of tiny feet. To all intents and purposes he would be a grandfather. Priding himself on his cunning, he kept his dream to himself, as he thought, but underestimated Ann's smartness.

For days together she would follow Matthew with her eyes, watching him from behind her long lashes, listening in silence to everything he said, vainly seeking to find points in him. He was unaware of her generous intentions. He had a vague feeling he was being criticised. He resented it even in those days.

"I do try," said Ann suddenly one evening apropos of nothing at all. "No one will ever know how hard I try not to dislike him."

Abner looked up.

"Sometimes," continued Ann, "I tell myself I have almost succeeded. And then he will go and do something that will bring it all on again."

"What does he do?" asked Abner.

"Oh, I can't tell you," confessed Ann. "If I told you it would sound as if it was my fault. It's all so silly. And then he thinks such a lot of himself. If one only knew why! He can't tell you himself when you ask him."

"You have asked him?" queried Abner.

"I wanted to know," explained Ann. "I thought there might be something in him that I could like."

"Why do you want to like him?" asked Abner, wondering how much she had guessed.

"I know," wailed Ann. "You are hoping that when I am grown up I shall marry him. And I don't want to. It's so ungrateful of me."

"Well, you're not grown up yet," Abner consoled her. "And so long as you are feeling like that about it, I'm not likely to want you to marry him."

"It would make you so happy," sobbed Ann.

"Yes, but we've got to think of the boy, don't forget that," laughed Abner. "Perhaps he might object."

"He would. I know he would," cried Ann with conviction. "He's no better than I am."

"Have you been asking him to?" demanded Abner, springing up from his chair.

"Not to marry me," explained Ann. "But I told him he must be an unnatural little beast not to try to like me when he knew how you loved me."

"Helpful way of putting it," growled Abner. "And what did he say to that?"

"Admitted it," flashed Ann indignantly. "Said he had tried."

Abner succeeded in persuading her that the path of dignity and virtue lay in her dismissing the whole subject from her mind.

He had made a mistake, so he told himself. Age may be attracted by contrast, but youth has no use for its opposite. He would send Matthew away. He could return for week-ends. Continually so close to one another, they saw only one another's specks and flaws; there is no beauty without perspective. Matthew wanted the corners rubbed off him, that was all. Mixing more with men, his priggishness would be laughed out of him. Otherwise he was quite a decent youngster, clean minded, high principled. Clever, too: he often said quite unexpected things. With approaching womanhood, changes were taking place in Ann. Seeing her every day one hardly noticed them; but there were times when, standing before him flushed from a walk or bending over him to kiss him before starting for some friendly dance, Abner would blink his eyes and be puzzled. The thin arms were growing round and firm; the sallow complexion warming into olive; the once patchy, mouse-coloured hair darkening into a rich harmony of brown. The eyes beneath her level brows, that had always been her charm, still reminded Abner of her mother; but there was more light in them, more danger.

"I'll run down to Albany and talk to Jephson about him," decided Abner. "He can come home on Saturdays."

The plot might have succeeded: one never can tell. But a New York blizzard put a stop to it. The cars broke down, and Abner, walking home in thin shoes from a meeting, caught a chill, which, being neglected, proved fatal.

Abner was troubled as he lay upon his bed. The children were sitting very silent by the window. He sent Matthew out on a message, and then beckoned Ann to come to him. He loved the boy, too, but Ann was nearer to him.

"You haven't thought any more," he whispered, "about--"

"No," answered Ann. "You wished me not to."

"You must never think," he said, "to show your love for my memory by doing anything that would not make you happy. If I am anywhere around," he continued with a smile, "it will be your good I shall be watching for, not my own way. You will remember that?"

He had meant to do more for them, but the end had come so much sooner than he had expected. To Ann he left the house (Mrs. Travers had already retired on a small pension) and a sum that, judiciously invested, the friend and attorney thought should be sufficient for her needs, even supposing--The friend and attorney, pausing to dwell upon the oval face with its dark eyes, left the sentence unfinished.

To Matthew he wrote a loving letter, enclosing a thousand dollars. He knew that Matthew, now in a position to earn his living as a journalist, would rather have taken nothing. It was to be looked upon merely as a parting gift. Matthew decided to spend it on travel. It would fit him the better for his journalistic career, so he explained to Ann. But in his heart he had other ambitions. It would enable him to put them to the test.

So there came an evening when Ann stood waving a handkerchief as a great liner cast its moorings. She watched it till its lights grew dim, and then returned to West Twentieth Street. Strangers would take possession of it on the morrow. Ann had her supper in the kitchen in company with the nurse, who had stayed on at her request; and that night, slipping noiselessly from her room, she lay upon the floor, her head resting against the arm of the chair where Abner had been wont to sit and smoke his evening pipe; somehow it seemed to comfort her. And Matthew the while, beneath the stars, was pacing the silent deck of the great liner and planning out the future.

To only one other being had he ever confided his dreams. She lay in the churchyard; and there was nothing left to encourage him but his own heart. But he had no doubts. He would be a great writer. His two hundred pounds would support him till he had gained a foothold. After that he would climb swiftly. He had done right, so he told himself, to turn his back on journalism: the grave of literature. He would see men and cities, writing as he went. Looking back, years later, he was able to congratulate himself on having chosen the right road. He thought it would lead him by easy ascent to fame and fortune. It did better for him than that. It led him through poverty and loneliness, through hope deferred and heartache--through long nights of fear, when pride and confidence fell upon him, leaving him only the courage to endure.

His great poems, his brilliant essays, had been rejected so often that even he himself had lost all love for them. At the suggestion of an editor more kindly than the general run, and urged by need, he had written some short pieces of a less ambitious nature. It was in bitter disappointment he commenced them, regarding them as mere pot-boilers. He would not give them his name. He signed them "Aston Rowant." It was the name of the village in Oxfordshire where he had been born. It occurred to him by chance. It would serve the purpose as well as another. As the work progressed it grew upon him. He made his stories out of incidents and people he had seen; everyday comedies and tragedies that he had lived among, of things that he had felt; and when after their appearance in the magazine a publisher was found willing to make them into a book, hope revived in him.

It was but short-lived. The few reviews that reached him contained nothing but ridicule. So he had no place even as a literary hack!

He was living in Paris at the time in a noisy, evil-smelling street leading out of the Quai Saint-Michel. He thought of Chatterton, and would loaf on the bridges looking down into the river where the drowned lights twinkled.

And then one day there came to him a letter, sent on to him from the publisher of his one book. It was signed "Sylvia," nothing else, and bore no address. Matthew picked up the envelope. The postmark was "London, S.E."

It was a childish letter. A prosperous, well-fed genius, familiar with such, might have smiled at it. To Matthew in his despair it brought healing. She had found the book lying in an empty railway carriage; and undeterred by moral scruples had taken it home with her. It had remained forgotten for a time, until when the end really seemed to have come her hand by chance had fallen on it. She fancied some kind little wandering spirit--the spirit perhaps of someone who had known what it was to be lonely and very sad and just about broken almost--must have manoeuvred the whole thing. It had seemed to her as though some strong and gentle hand had been laid upon her in the darkness. She no longer felt friendless. And so on.

The book, he remembered, contained a reference to the magazine in which the sketches had first appeared. She would be sure to have noticed this. He would send her his answer. He drew his chair up to the flimsy table, and all that night he wrote.

He did not have to think. It came to him, and for the first time since the beginning of things he had no fear of its not being accepted. It was mostly about himself, and the rest was about her, but to most of those who read it two months later it seemed to be about themselves. The editor wrote a charming letter, thanking him for it; but at the time the chief thing that worried him was whether "Sylvia" had seen it. He waited anxiously for a few weeks, and then received her second letter. It was a more womanly letter than the first. She had understood the story, and her words of thanks almost conveyed to him the flush of pleasure with which she had read it. His friendship, she confessed, would be very sweet to her, and still more delightful the thought that he had need of her: that she also had something to give. She would write, as he wished, her real thoughts and feelings. They would never know one another, and that would give her boldness. They would be comrades, meeting only in dreamland.

In this way commenced the whimsical romance of Sylvia and Aston Rowant; for it was too late now to change the name--it had become a name to conjure with. The stories, poems, and essays followed now in regular succession. The anxiously expected letters reached him in orderly procession. They grew in interest, in helpfulness. They became the letters of a wonderfully sane, broad-minded, thoughtful woman--a woman of insight, of fine judgment. Their praise was rare enough to be precious. Often they would contain just criticism, tempered by sympathy, lightened by humour. Of her troubles, sorrows, fears, she came to write less and less, and even then not until they were past and she could laugh at them. The subtlest flattery she gave him was the suggestion that he had taught her to put these things into their proper place. Intimate, self-revealing as her letters were, it was curious he never shaped from them any satisfactory image of the writer.

A brave, kind, tender woman. A self-forgetting, quickly-forgiving woman. A many-sided woman, responding to joy, to laughter: a merry lady, at times. Yet by no means a perfect woman. There could be flashes of temper, one felt that; quite often occasional unreasonableness; a tongue that could be cutting. A sweet, restful, greatly loving woman, but still a woman: it would be wise to remember that. So he read her from her letters. But herself, the eyes, and hair, and lips of her, the voice and laugh and smile of her, the hands and feet of her, always they eluded him.

He was in Alaska one spring, where he had gone to collect material for his work, when he received the last letter she ever wrote him. They neither of them knew then it would be the last. She was leaving London, so the postscript informed him, sailing on the following Saturday for New York, where for the future she intended to live.

It worried him that postscript. He could not make out for a long time why it worried him. Suddenly, in a waste of endless snows, the explanation flashed across him. Sylvia of the letters was a living woman! She could travel--with a box, he supposed, possibly with two or three, and parcels. Could take tickets, walk up a gangway, stagger about a deck feeling, maybe, a little seasick. All these years he had been living with her in dreamland she had been, if he had only known it, a Miss Somebody-or-other, who must have stood every morning in front of a looking-glass with hairpins in her mouth. He had never thought of her doing these things; it shocked him. He could not help feeling it was indelicate of her--coming to life in this sudden, uncalled-for manner.

He struggled with this new conception of her, and had almost forgiven her, when a further and still more startling suggestion arrived to plague him. If she really lived why should he not see her, speak to her? So long as she had remained in her hidden temple, situate in the vague recesses of London, S.E., her letters had contented him. But now that she had moved, now that she was no longer a voice but a woman! Well, it would be interesting to see what she was like. He imagined the introduction: "Miss Somebody- or-other, allow me to present you to Mr. Matthew Pole." She would have no idea he was Aston Rowant. If she happened to be young, beautiful, in all ways satisfactory, he would announce himself. How astonished, how delighted she would be.

But if not! If she were elderly, plain? The wisest, wittiest of women have been known to have an incipient moustache. A beautiful spirit can, and sometimes does, look out of goggle eyes. Suppose she suffered from indigestion and had a shiny nose! Would her letters ever again have the same charm for him? Absurd that they should not. But would they?

The risk was too great. Giving the matter long and careful consideration, he decided to send her back into dreamland.

But somehow she would not go back into dreamland, would persist in remaining in New York, a living, breathing woman.

Yet even so, how could he find her? He might, say, in a poem convey to her his desire for a meeting. Would she comply? And if she did, what would be his position, supposing the inspection to result unfavourably for her?

Could he, in effect, say to her: "Thank you for letting me have a look at you; that is all I wanted. Good-bye"?

She must, she should remain in dreamland. He would forget her postscript; in future throw her envelopes unglanced at into the wastepaper basket. Having by this simple exercise of his will replaced her in London, he himself started for New York--on his way back to Europe, so he told himself. Still, being in New York, there was no reason for not lingering there a while, if merely to renew old memories.

Of course, if he had really wanted to find Sylvia it would have been easy from the date upon the envelope to have discovered the ship "sailing the following Saturday." Passengers were compelled to register their names in full, and to state their intended movements after arrival in America. Sylvia was not a common Christian name. By the help of a five-dollar bill or two--. The idea had not occurred to him before. He dismissed it from his mind and sought a quiet hotel up town.

New York was changed less than he had anticipated. West Twentieth Street in particular was precisely as, leaning out of the cab window, he had looked back upon it ten years ago. Business had more and more taken possession of it, but had not as yet altered its appearance. His conscience smote him as he turned the corner that he had never once written to Ann. He had meant to, it goes without saying, but during those first years of struggle and failure his pride had held him back. She had always thought him a fool; he had felt she did. He would wait till he could write to her of success, of victory. And then when it had slowly, almost imperceptibly, arrived--! He wondered why he never had. Quite a nice little girl, in some respects. If only she had been less conceited, less self-willed. Also rather a pretty girl she had shown signs of becoming. There were times-- He remembered an evening before the lamps were lighted. She had fallen asleep curled up in Abner's easy chair, one small hand resting upon the arm. She had always had quite attractive hands--a little too thin. Something had moved him to steal across softly without waking her. He smiled at the memory.

And then her eyes, beneath the level brows! It was surprising how Ann was coming back to him. Perhaps they would be able to tell him, the people of the house, what had become of her. If they were decent people they would let him wander round a while. He would explain that he had lived there in Abner Herrick's time. The room where they had sometimes been agreeable to one another while Abner, pretending to read, had sat watching them out of the corner of an eye. He would like to sit there for a few moments, by himself.

He forgot that he had rung the bell. A very young servant had answered the door and was staring at him. He would have walked in if the small servant had not planted herself deliberately in his way. It recalled him to himself.

"I beg pardon," said Matthew, "but would you please tell me who lives here?"

The small servant looked him up and down with growing suspicion.

"Miss Kavanagh lives here," she said. "What do you want?"

The surprise was so great it rendered him speechless. In another moment the small servant would have slammed the door.

"Miss Ann Kavanagh?" he inquired, just in time.

"That's her name," admitted the small servant, less suspicious.

"Will you please tell her Mr. Pole--Mr. Matthew Pole," he requested.

"I'll see first if she is in," said the small servant, and shut the door.

It gave Matthew a few minutes to recover himself, for which he was glad. Then the door opened again suddenly.

"You are to come upstairs," said the small servant.

It sounded so like Ann that it quite put him at his ease. He followed the small servant up the stairs.

"Mr. Matthew Pole," she announced severely, and closed the door behind him.

Ann was standing by the window and came to meet him. It was in front of Abner's empty chair that they shook hands.

"So you have come back to the old house," said Matthew.

"Yes," she answered. "It never let well. The last people who had it gave it up at Christmas. It seemed the best thing to do, even from a purely economical point of view.

"What have you been doing all these years?" she asked him.

"Oh, knocking about," he answered. "Earning my living." He was curious to discover what she thought of Matthew, first of all.

"It seems to have agreed with you," she commented, with a glance that took him in generally, including his clothes.

"Yes," he answered. "I have had more luck than perhaps I deserved."

"I am glad of that," said Ann.

He laughed. "So you haven't changed so very much," he said. "Except in appearance."

"Isn't that the most important part of a woman?" suggested Ann.

"Yes," he answered, thinking. "I suppose it is."

She was certainly very beautiful.

"How long are you stopping in New York?" she asked him.

"Oh, not long," he explained.

"Don't leave it for another ten years," she said, "before letting me know what is happening to you. We didn't get on very well together as children; but we mustn't let him think we're not friends. It would hurt him."

She spoke quite seriously, as if she were expecting him any moment to open the door and join them. Involuntarily Matthew glanced round the room. Nothing seemed altered. The worn carpet, the faded curtains, Abner's easy chair, his pipe upon the corner of the mantelpiece beside the vase of spills.

"It is curious," he said, "finding this vein of fancy, of tenderness in you. I always regarded you as such a practical, unsentimental young person."

"Perhaps we neither of us knew each other too well, in those days," she answered.

The small servant entered with the tea.

"What have you been doing with yourself?" he asked, drawing his chair up to the table.

She waited till the small servant had withdrawn.

"Oh, knocking about," she answered. "Earning my living."

"It seems to have agreed with you," he repeated, smiling.

"It's all right now," she answered. "It was a bit of a struggle at first."

"Yes," he agreed. "Life doesn't temper the wind to the human lamb. But was there any need in your case?" he asked. "I thought--"

"Oh, that all went," she explained. "Except the house."

"I'm sorry," said Matthew. "I didn't know."

"Oh, we have been a couple of pigs," she laughed, replying to his thoughts. "I did sometimes think of writing you. I kept the address you gave me. Not for any assistance; I wanted to fight it out for myself. But I was a bit lonely."

"Why didn't you?" he asked.

She hesitated for a moment.

"It's rather soon to make up one's mind," she said, "but you seem to me to have changed. Your voice sounds so different. But as a boy-- well, you were a bit of a prig, weren't you? I imagined you writing me good advice and excellent short sermons. And it wasn't that that I was wanting."

"I think I understand," he said. "I'm glad you got through.

"What is your line?" he asked. "Journalism?"

"No," she answered. "Too self-opinionated."

She opened a bureau that had always been her own and handed him a programme. "Miss Ann Kavanagh, Contralto," was announced on it as one of the chief attractions.

"I didn't know you had a voice," said Matthew.

"You used to complain of it," she reminded him.

"Your speaking voice," he corrected her. "And it wasn't the quality of that I objected to. It was the quantity."

She laughed.

"Yes, we kept ourselves pretty busy bringing one another up," she admitted.

They talked a while longer: of Abner and his kind, quaint ways; of old friends. Ann had lost touch with most of them. She had studied singing in Brussels, and afterwards her master had moved to London and she had followed him. She had only just lately returned to New York.

The small servant entered to clear away the tea things. She said she thought that Ann had rung. Her tone implied that anyhow it was time she had. Matthew rose and Ann held out her hand.

"I shall be at the concert," he said.

"It isn't till next week," Ann reminded him.

"Oh, I'm not in any particular hurry," said Matthew. "Are you generally in of an afternoon?"

"Sometimes," said Ann.

He thought as he sat watching her from his stall that she was one of the most beautiful women he had ever seen. Her voice was not great. She had warned him not to expect too much.

"It will never set the Thames on fire," she had said. "I thought at first that it would. But such as it is I thank God for it."

It was worth that. It was sweet and clear and had a tender quality.

Matthew waited for her at the end. She was feeling well disposed towards all creatures and accepted his suggestion of supper with gracious condescension.

He had called on her once or twice during the preceding days. It was due to her after his long neglect of her, he told himself, and had found improvement in her. But to-night she seemed to take a freakish pleasure in letting him see that there was much of the old Ann still left in her: the frank conceit of her; the amazing self-opinionatedness of her; the waywardness, the wilfulness, the unreasonableness of her; the general uppishness and dictatorialness of her; the contradictoriness and flat impertinence of her; the swift temper and exasperating tongue of her.

It was almost as if she were warning him. "You see, I am not changed, except, as you say, in appearance. I am still Ann with all the old faults and failings that once made life in the same house with me a constant trial to you. Just now my very imperfections appear charms. You have been looking at the sun--at the glory of my face, at the wonder of my arms and hands. Your eyes are blinded. But that will pass. And underneath I am still Ann. Just Ann."

They had quarrelled in the cab on the way home. He forgot what it was about, but Ann had said some quite rude things, and her face not being there in the darkness to excuse her, it had made him very angry. She had laughed again on the steps, and they had shaken hands. But walking home through the still streets Sylvia had plucked at his elbow.

What fools we mortals be--especially men! Here was a noble woman--a restful, understanding, tenderly loving woman; a woman as nearly approaching perfection as it was safe for a woman to go! This marvellous woman was waiting for him with outstretched arms (why should he doubt it?)--and just because Nature had at last succeeded in making a temporary success of Ann's skin and had fashioned a rounded line above her shoulder-blade! It made him quite cross with himself. Ten years ago she had been gawky and sallow-complexioned. Ten years hence she might catch the yellow jaundice and lose it all. Passages in Sylvia's letters returned to him. He remembered that far-off evening in his Paris attic when she had knocked at his door with her great gift of thanks. Recalled how her soft shadow hand had stilled his pain. He spent the next two days with Sylvia. He re-read all her letters, lived again the scenes and moods in which he had replied to them.

Her personality still defied the efforts of his imagination, but he ended by convincing himself that he would know her when he saw her. But counting up the women on Fifth Avenue towards whom he had felt instinctively drawn, and finding that the number had already reached eleven, began to doubt his intuition. On the morning of the third day he met Ann by chance in a bookseller's shop. Her back was towards him. She was glancing through Aston Rowant's latest volume.

"What I," said the cheerful young lady who was attending to her, "like about him is that he understands women so well."

"What I like about him," said Ann, "is that he doesn't pretend to."

"There's something in that," agreed the cheerful young lady. "They say he's here in New York."

Ann looked up.

"So I've been told," said the cheerful young lady.

"I wonder what he's like?" said Ann.

"He wrote for a long time under another name," volunteered the cheerful young lady. "He's quite an elderly man."

It irritated Matthew. He spoke without thinking.

"No, he isn't," he said. "He's quite young."

The ladies turned and looked at him.

"You know him?" queried Ann. She was most astonished, and appeared disbelieving. That irritated him further.

"If you care about it," he said. "I will introduce you to him."

Ann made no answer. He bought a copy of the book for himself, and they went out together. They turned towards the park.

Ann seemed thoughtful. "What is he doing here in New York?" she wondered.

"Looking for a lady named Sylvia," answered Matthew.

He thought the time was come to break it to her that he was a great and famous man. Then perhaps she would be sorry she had said what she had said in the cab. Seeing he had made up his mind that his relationship to her in the future would be that of an affectionate brother, there would be no harm in also letting her know about Sylvia. That also might be good for her.

They walked two blocks before Ann spoke. Matthew, anticipating a pleasurable conversation, felt no desire to hasten matters.

"How intimate are you with him?" she demanded. "I don't think he would have said that to a mere acquaintance."

"I'm not a mere acquaintance," said Matthew. "I've known him a long time."

"You never told me," complained Ann.

"Didn't know it would interest you," replied Matthew.

He waited for further questions, but they did not come. At Thirty- fourth Street he saved her from being run over and killed, and again at Forty-second Street. Just inside the park she stopped abruptly and held out her hand.

"Tell him," she replied, "that if he is really serious about finding Sylvia, I may--I don't say I can--but I may be able to help him."

He did not take her hand, but stood stock still in the middle of the path and stared at her.

"You!" he said. "You know her?"

She was prepared for his surprise. She was also prepared--not with a lie, that implies evil intention. Her only object was to have a talk with the gentleman and see what he was like before deciding on her future proceedings--let us say, with a plausible story.

"We crossed on the same boat," she said. "We found there was a good deal in common between us. She--she told me things." When you came to think it out it was almost the truth.

"What is she like?" demanded Matthew.

"Oh, just--well, not exactly--" It was an awkward question. There came to her relief the reflection that there was really no need for her to answer it.

"What's it got to do with you?" she said.

"I am Aston Rowant," said Matthew.

The Central Park, together with the universe in general, fell away and disappeared. Somewhere out of chaos was sounding a plaintive voice: "What is she like? Can't you tell me? Is she young or old?"

It seemed to have been going on for ages. She made one supreme gigantic effort, causing the Central Park to reappear, dimly, faintly, but it was there again. She was sitting on a seat. Matthew--Aston Rowant, whatever it was--was seated beside her.

"You've seen her? What is she like?"

"I can't tell you."

He was evidently very cross with her. It seemed so unkind of him.

"Why can't you tell me--or, why won't you tell me? Do you mean she's too awful for words?"

"No, certainly not--as a matter of fact--"

"Well, what?"

She felt she must get away or there would be hysterics somewhere. She sprang up and began to walk rapidly towards the gate. He followed her.

"I'll write you," said Ann.

"But why--?"

"I can't," said Ann. "I've got a rehearsal."

A car was passing. She made a dash for it and clambered on. Before he could make up his mind it had gathered speed.

Ann let herself in with her key. She called downstairs to the small servant that she wasn't to be disturbed for anything. She locked the door.

So it was to Matthew that for six years she had been pouring out her inmost thoughts and feelings! It was to Matthew that she had laid bare her tenderest, most sacred dreams! It was at Matthew's feet that for six years she had been sitting, gazing up with respectful admiration, with reverential devotion! She recalled her letters, almost passage for passage, till she had to hold her hands to her face to cool it. Her indignation, one might almost say fury, lasted till tea-time.

In the evening--it was in the evening time that she had always written to him--a more reasonable frame of mind asserted itself. After all, it was hardly his fault. He couldn't have known who she was. He didn't know now. She had wanted to write. Without doubt he had helped her, comforted her loneliness; had given her a charming friendship, a delightful comradeship. Much of his work had been written for her, to her. It was fine work. She had been proud of her share in it. Even allowing there were faults--irritability, shortness of temper, a tendency to bossiness!--underneath it all was a man. The gallant struggle, the difficulties overcome, the long suffering, the high courage--all that she, reading between the lines, had divined of his life's battle! Yes, it was a man she had worshipped. A woman need not be ashamed of that. As Matthew he had seemed to her conceited, priggish. As Aston Rowant she wondered at his modesty, his patience.

And all these years he had been dreaming of her; had followed her to New York; had--

There came a sudden mood so ludicrous, so absurdly unreasonable that Ann herself stopped to laugh at it. Yet it was real, and it hurt. He had come to New York thinking of Sylvia, yearning for Sylvia. He had come to New York with one desire: to find Sylvia. And the first pretty woman that had come across his path had sent Sylvia clean out of his head. There could be no question of that. When Ann Kavanagh stretched out her hand to him in that very room a fortnight ago he had stood before her dazzled, captured. From that moment Sylvia had been tossed aside and forgotten. Ann Kavanagh could have done what she liked with him. She had quarrelled with him that evening of the concert. She had meant to quarrel with him.

And then for the first time he had remembered Sylvia. That was her reward--Sylvia's: it was Sylvia she was thinking of--for six years' devoted friendship; for the help, the inspiration she had given him.

As Sylvia, she suffered from a very genuine and explainable wave of indignant jealousy. As Ann, she admitted he ought not to have done it, but felt there was excuse for him. Between the two she feared her mind would eventually give way. On the morning of the second day she sent Matthew a note asking him to call in the afternoon. Sylvia might be there, or she might not. She would mention it to her.

She dressed herself in a quiet, dark-coloured frock. It seemed uncommittal and suitable to the occasion. It also happened to be the colour that best suited her. She would not have the lamps lighted.

Matthew arrived in a dark serge suit and a blue necktie, so that the general effect was quiet. Ann greeted him with kindliness and put him with his face to what little light there was. She chose for herself the window-seat. Sylvia had not arrived. She might be a little late--that is, if she came at all.

They talked about the weather for a while. Matthew was of opinion they were going to have some rain. Ann, who was in one of her contradictory moods, thought there was frost in the air.

"What did you say to her?" he asked.

"Sylvia? Oh, what you told me," replied Ann. "That you had come to New York to--to look for her."

"What did she say?" he asked.

"Said you'd taken your time about it," retorted Ann.

Matthew looked up with an injured expression.

"It was her own idea that we should never meet," he explained.

"Um!" Ann grunted.

"What do you think yourself she will be like?" she continued. "Have you formed any notion?"

"It is curious," he replied. "I have never been able to conjure up any picture of her until just now."

"Why 'just now'?" demanded Ann.

"I had an idea I should find her here when I opened the door," he answered. "You were standing in the shadow. It seemed to be just what I had expected."

"You would have been satisfied?" she asked.

"Yes," he said.

There was silence for a moment.

"Uncle Ab made a mistake," he continued. "He ought to have sent me away. Let me come home now and then."

"You mean," said Ann, "that if you had seen less of me you might have liked me better?"

"Quite right," he admitted. "We never see the things that are always there."

"A thin, gawky girl with a bad complexion," she suggested. "Would it have been of any use?"

"You must always have been wonderful with those eyes," he answered. "And your hands were beautiful even then."

"I used to cry sometimes when I looked at myself in the glass as a child," she confessed. "My hands were the only thing that consoled me."

"I kissed them once," he told her. "You were asleep, curled up in Uncle Ab's chair."

"I wasn't asleep," said Ann.

She was seated with one foot tucked underneath her. She didn't look a bit grown up.

"You always thought me a fool," he said.

"It used to make me so angry with you," said Ann, "that you seemed to have no go, no ambition in you. I wanted you to wake up--do something. If I had known you were a budding genius--"

"I did hint it to you," said he.

"Oh, of course it was all my fault," said Ann.

He rose. "You think she means to come?" he asked. Ann also had risen.

"Is she so very wonderful?" she asked.

"I may be exaggerating to myself," he answered. "But I am not sure that I could go on with my work without her--not now."

"You forgot her," flashed Ann, "till we happened to quarrel in the cab."

"I often do," he confessed. "Till something goes wrong. Then she comes to me. As she did on that first evening, six years ago. You see, I have been more or less living with her since then," he added with a smile.

"In dreamland," Ann corrected.

"Yes, but in my case," he answered, "the best part of my life is passed in dreamland."

"And when you are not in dreamland?" she demanded. "When you're just irritable, short-tempered, cranky Matthew Pole. What's she going to do about you then?"

"She'll put up with me," said Matthew.

"No she won't," said Ann. "She'll snap your head off. Most of the 'putting up with' you'll have to do."

He tried to get between her and the window, but she kept her face close to the pane.

"You make me tired with Sylvia," she said. "It's about time you did know what she's like. She's just the commonplace, short-tempered, disagreeable-if-she-doesn't-get-her-own-way, unreasonable woman. Only more so."

He drew her away from the window by brute force.

"So you're Sylvia," he said.

"I thought that would get it into your head," said Ann.

It was not at all the way she had meant to break it to him. She had meant the conversation to be chiefly about Sylvia. She had a high opinion of Sylvia, a much higher opinion than she had of Ann Kavanagh. If he proved to be worthy of her--of Sylvia, that is, then, with the whimsical smile that she felt belonged to Sylvia, she would remark quite simply, "Well, what have you got to say to her?"

What had happened to interfere with the programme was Ann Kavanagh. It seemed that Ann Kavanagh had disliked Matthew Pole less than she had thought she did. It was after he had sailed away that little Ann Kavanagh had discovered this. If only he had shown a little more interest in, a little more appreciation of, Ann Kavanagh! He could be kind and thoughtful in a patronising sort of way. Even that would not have mattered if there had been any justification for his airs of superiority.

Ann Kavanagh, who ought to have taken a back seat on this occasion, had persisted in coming to the front. It was so like her.

"Well," she said, "what are you going to say to her?" She did get it in, after all.

"I was going," said Matthew, "to talk to her about Art and Literature, touching, maybe, upon a few other subjects. Also, I might have suggested our seeing each other again once or twice, just to get better acquainted. And then I was going away."

"Why going away?" asked Ann.

"To see if I could forget you."

She turned to him. The fading light was full upon her face.

"I don't believe you could--again," she said.

"No," he agreed. "I'm afraid I couldn't."

"You're sure there's nobody else," said Ann, "that you're in love with. Only us two?"

"Only you two," he said.

She was standing with her hand on old Abner's empty chair. "You've got to choose," she said. She was trembling. Her voice sounded just a little hard.

He came and stood beside her. "I want Ann," he said.

She held out her hand to him.

"I'm so glad you said Ann," she laughed.


-THE END-